LAURA OWEN & KORKY PAUL

Winnie and Wilbur

Spooky
WINNIE

OXFORD
UNIVERSITY PRESS

CONTENTS

WINNIE'S
Time Machine

7

WINNIE
the Shadowitch

29

Troublesome
WANDS

53

Spooky
WINNIE

75

WINNIE'S
Time Machine

Winnie looked at her garden, and sighed.
'That flower bed looks like a noodle-
doodle salad with added slugs on the side.
Still, it'll look better when I've planted this
nice lolly-lily plant. And it'll give me fresh
lollies to pick all summer long! Now, what
can I find for the lolly-lily plant to grow
up?'

Winnie stuck her spade into the earth,
and was about to dig when,

Crash! Ting! Ping!

'Oh dear, oh no, oh blow!'

'That's Jerry next door,' said Winnie to Wilbur. 'Come on, catman, let's see what he's up to.'

High over the fence leapt Winnie the Witch, and Wilbur scrabbled over after her. They opened Jerry's giant front door,

8

and—*sploosh!*—out swept Scruff the
dog, surfing a frothy warm wave of water.

'What in the witchy world?' began
Winnie.

'It's me washing machine,
Missus,' said Jerry, squelching through
a soggy pile of clothes. 'I was just
washing me smalls when me
machine started banging.

I couldn't find me hammer, so
I gave it a tap with me mallet
instead and, well . . . it's broke!
I've got nuffink to wear now!'

'I'll do your washing in my machine if
you like,' said Winnie. Wilbur put his head
in his paws, but,

'Oh, fanks, Missus!' said Jerry.

Winnie had forgotten that Jerry's smalls
weren't small at all. Jerry's smalls were huge!

10

'It only takes three of his great soggy pongy socks to completely fill my little machine,' said Winnie. **Squirt-slosh-churn-rattle-sigh-clunk!** went her washing machine as it worked on the giant socks. 'How am I going to fit all his other clothes into it?' she wondered.

Then Winnie pulled out something from a pocket in Jerry's huge overalls. 'It's Jerry's hammer! No wonder his machine was banging!'

Worse than doing all the washing was hanging it up to dry. Wilbur helped Winnie to heave a giant shirt the size of a sofa cover onto her washing line. The sleeves trailed into the dirt because it was so big, and then—

TWANG!

—the washing line collapsed under the weight.

'Jitterbug juice jelly, the whole blooming lot is dirty again!' said Winnie. 'Jerry!' she shrieked. 'You'll have to put up a new washing line for us!'

13

Jerry tied a washing line between two
tree tops, then Winnie and Wilbur flew up
on the broom to peg his pants and socks
and hankies and shirts.

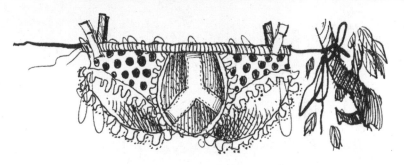

'I never knew you wore such fancy
pants!' said Winnie, and Wilbur snickered
behind a paw as Jerry blushed as red as a
squashed tomato. 'There!' said Winnie,
standing back to admire her work. 'All
done!'

Flash! Thunder! Rumble!

'Oh, no!' said Winnie. 'Please don't
rain!' But it did rain, very hard.

'How's the washing going to get dry
now?' said Winnie. 'Poor Jerry's shivering
with cold. He needs some clothes, and
none of my clothes would fit him, even if
he did want to borrow a purple dress.'

Winnie shook rain from her hair.
'Honestly!' said Winnie. 'I've got a
machine to wash clothes, a machine to
toast toadstool crumpets, machines for just
about everything. But what I really need
now is a machine to . . .' She was about
to say, 'dry the washing', when Wilbur
pointed at the clock.

'Meow!' he said. It was time for his
favourite *Mice in the Attic* television
programme. But the clock made Winnie
think of something else.

'Wilbur, you're a genius!' she said.
'That's it! We'll make a machine to turn
the time back to *before* Jerry broke his
washing machine. Then everything will be
hunky-snory!'

They gathered chairs and levers and
knobs and buttons, and the clock, of
course.

'Stand back!' said Winnie, waving her
wand, *'Abracadabra!'*

CLATTER-CLUNK-CLUNK!

'Behold a monstrously magnificent marvellous time machine!' announced Winnie. They put on cauldron smash helmets and climbed into the machine.

'Right,' said Winnie. 'Set it for eight o'clock this morning.' Wilbur was just setting the clock when . . .

A flash of lightning made them all jump and Wilbur's clock-setting went a bit haywire.

ZOOM! SHAKE! RATTLE AND ROLL!

They were speeding through time and space.

19

'W-w-w-where, or w-w-w-when, are we going to, I w-w-w-wonder?' said Winnie, clutching on tight.

'D-d-d-dunno, Missus!' said Jerry.

Bump! They landed in a damp dark cave.

'Ooer-er-er!' said Winnie, her voice echoing. 'Wherever are we-we-we?'

'Meow!' Wilbur pointed to where a fire was burning at the cave entrance. 'Goodee-ee-ee,' said Winnie and her echo. 'There must be somebody here-ere-ere-ere.'

But they couldn't see anybody. Just a drawing on the cave wall.

'Whoever lives here has a cat,' said Winnie. 'And a dog. So they must be ever so friendly!'

21

'They's got giant h'animals!'
said Jerry, picking up some huge bones.

Gulp! went Wilbur, pointing a claw
at something, or somebody, in the cave
opening.

'Er, I fink it might be time
to go, Missus,' said Jerry because the
person at the cave entrance didn't look
ever so friendly after all. She was holding a
spear!

22

'Oggle-bog-flog!' shouted the cave woman, just as the ground started to shake and a huge hairy mammoth went running by with a whole lot of men and funny-looking cats chasing after it.

'Er, time to go home, and quick!' said Winnie. 'Hold tight!' Winnie waved her wand, 'Abracadabra!'

Whirl-swirl-twirl-clatter.

They landed back in Winnie's kitchen with the rain still splattering the windows.

'Safe and sound!' said Winnie. 'But what was all that clattering?'

'It was them bones,' said Jerry. 'They came back wiv me.'

24

'Hmm, I wonder what kind of critter they belonged to?' said Winnie. 'Let's see.' Winnie waved her wand, '*Abracadabra!*'

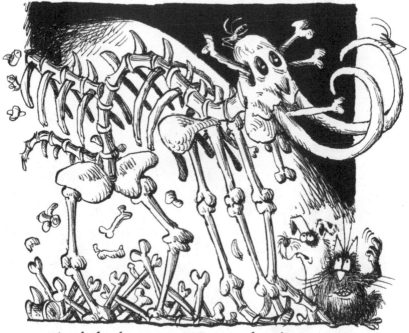

And the bones came together in a rather odd-looking way.

'Oh! I don't think five legs and two tails can be right, can it?' said Winnie.

She waved her wand again. '*Abracadabra!*'

'That's not right either.'

Another wave. '*Abracadabra!* Ooh, it's a mega-mammoth skellington!' said Winnie.

A mammoth skeleton made the perfect clothes rack for drying giant-sized clothes.

After all that adventure, Winnie planted
her lolly-lily, and it turned out that a
mammoth skeleton is just what you need
for a lolly-lily plant to grow up.

28

WINNIE
the Shadowitch

One dark evening, Winnie clicked the switch to turn on her lights, but everything stayed dark.

'The power's gone off!' said Winnie. 'We'll have to use Wee Willie Winkie candles until it's on again.'

Winnie and Wilbur weren't sure what they ate for supper. They could hardly see what they were cooking or eating in the flickering candlelight.

'Well, that meal was a culinary mystery tour,' said Winnie, picking bits from between her teeth. 'Now, what shall we do with our evening, Wilbur?' They couldn't watch telly or see well enough to read. But Winnie had another way to share a story with Wilbur. 'I know, I'll tell you a ghost story,' she said.

Wilbur got ready to listen.

'Once upon a time,' began Winnie.
She lifted her arms dramatically, and her
shadow on the wall suddenly became a
huge pouncing shape. Wilbur's fur went
up on end. On went Winnie. 'Once upon
a time there was a big dark house full of
creaks and groans and spiders and rats.

31

Just like this house, really.' Winnie leant over, and made her voice whispery. 'But the story house was in a wild wood full of whooshy wind and wailing bats. It was as dark as liquorice leeches.'

Wilbur shivered, eyes as big as mushrooms.

'And in this house a cat lived all on his little-old owny-oh,' said Winnie. 'That cat was called Tiddles.'

Wilbur rolled his eyes, but Winnie carried on.

'One dark day, Tiddles heard a **scratch-scritch-scratch.** Just the mice under the floor, thought Tiddles.

But the sound came again. **Scratch-scritch-scratch.** And it wasn't coming from under the floor now. It was coming from above his head. It must be  rats in the roof, thought Tiddles. But then the scratching came again, right behind him and louder than ever. **Scratch-scritch-scratch.** Tiddles felt a tap on his shoulder, and he turned and saw . . .'

'**Hiss!**' went Wilbur.

'. . . a ghost! And the ghost said, "So
sorry to disturb you, Tiddles my old fruit
bat, but I've got this terrible itch in the
middle of my back, and I just can't reach
the spot however much I scratch. Will you
scratch it for me?"'

'Meow!' said Wilbur.

'You're right,' said Winnie. 'It was a silly story. Bedtime now. Up we go.'

But the staircase was dark and dithery in the candlelight.

'Oo, this is spooky!' said Winnie, as she felt her way onto the first step. Her candlelight lurched around the family portraits all the way up. Their eyes seemed to follow her and their mouths seemed to leer and cackle. 'Horrible, aren't they,' whispered Winnie.

36

By the time they got to the top of the stairs, Winnie's and Wilbur's knees were knocking like a pocket full of eyeball marbles. As they hurried to bed, Winnie said, 'Let's paint some nice new portraits in the morning, and put them up the stairs instead. Nice pictures of us and our friends.'

'Purr!' agreed Wilbur.

So, next morning, Winnie got out paints
and paper and easels and overalls, and she
took them all outside into the sunshine.
'You paint me, and I'll paint you,' she told
Wilbur.

Splash-splat-whoops-splot!

'Er, this doesn't look much like you, Wilbur,' said Winnie. 'Do you mind if it looks a bit, well, a bit, um, "modern"?'

'Mrrow!' said Wilbur when he saw it.

'That bad, eh?' said Winnie. Then she

had a look at the picture Wilbur had
just finished. It was a bit of a splatty cat
scribble. 'I don't look anything like that
. . . do I?' said Winnie. 'This painting
lark isn't as easy as it looks. Perhaps . . .'
Winnie reached for her wand.

'Meow!' Wilbur had a different idea.

41

He held up a paw to make Winnie stand
absolutely still. Then he put some paper
on the ground behind her. Next, he dipped
his tail into the pot of beetle-boot black
paint, and he carefully ran the end of his
tail all around the edge of Winnie's shadow
as it lay on the paper. From the tip of her
nose, along and up and round and down,
in and out and up and down until he got
back to her nose again to join up the line.

'Wow, Wilbur!' said Winnie. 'That is
one good-looking witch!'

Wilbur coloured it in.

43

'Well, we've got at least one good
picture for the stairs,' said Winnie. 'Now
it's my turn to do you.'

Wilbur posed, and Winnie painted
around the outline of his shadow on the
paper. Then she filled it in with black, all
except for two big green eyes and blue
triangle ears. Then she added a pink nose
and some whiskers.

'Purrr!' said Wilbur when he saw it.

They called Jerry and Scruff over from
next door.

'There's just time to do Jerry before we
stop for lunch,' said Winnie. 'We'll need a
whole roll of wallpaper to fit a giant on!'

But, strangely, Jerry's shadow picture
came out shorter than Winnie expected.

'Ooer,' said Winnie. 'Jerry's not much
bigger than you, Wilbur!'

'Is I?' said Jerry, scratching his head.
'Is I smaller than you, Winnie?'

'Yes!' said Winnie. 'You've shrunk
yourself! It must be you doing the magic
today Jerry because I haven't touched my
wand!'

'So I is small *and* magical!' said
Jerry with a giant grin.

As the afternoon went on, Mrs Parmar
came to be painted, and some of the little
ordinaries, and Winnie's three sisters. 'All
my best people!' said Winnie. The strange
thing was that Jerry's magic seemed to
be working in the opposite direction as
afternoon turned to evening. Some of the
little ordinaries came out as giants. They
liked that!

Mrs Parmar clapped her hands. 'You
can tell your science teacher that you've
learned all about how shadows are longer
in the morning and evening and shorter
in the middle of the day!' she said bossily,
as she ushered the little ordinaries out of
Winnie's garden.

So the truth was that Jerry hadn't actually shrunk himself at all! Which was just as well when it came to hanging the pictures up the side of Winnie's staircase. They needed a proper *giant* giant to do that!

'Brillaramaroodles!' said Winnie, as she looked at the pictures. 'That looks as perfect as a tarantula in a tutu! I shall smile when I go up the stairs now, even if the blooming power goes off again and we need to use wobbly candlelight!'

Troublesome
WANDS

Winnie saw herself in the hall mirror, and
sighed.

'Just look at that scraggy old hair!
Maybe I should put it up today? In a bun?
In a croissant? In a doughnut? What do
you think, Wilbur?'

Wilbur yawned. Then—**plop!**—
something was pushed through the letter
flap, which immediately began munching
it.

53

'Oi! Stop eating that, you naughty letter flap!' said Winnie, grabbing the envelope. She pulled out a card with fancy-nancy twiddly-twirly writing on it.

'A witchogram!' said Winnie. The card wiffled with nasty smells and seemed to bubble in her hand.

54

Luckily for Winnie, who wasn't at all good at reading, witchograms always read themselves out loud in witchy voices.

Winnie the Witch,
You are invited to come to
THE ANNUAL WITCHES' SPELLING
COMPETITION
Held at
SCRATCHY BOTTOM HALL
this Friday 13th R.S.V.P.

INVITATIO

'Meow?' asked Wilbur, pointing at the RSVP.

'That means "reply soon (to be) very polite",' explained Winnie. 'I'll say "no". I don't like spelling tests.' So Winnie fed the card back to the letter flap. Then she felt in her cardigan pocket for her wand to send her reply witchogram. But her wand wasn't there. It wasn't in her dress pocket or her knickers pocket either. It wasn't *anywhere*.

'I had it just one maggoty minute ago!' wailed Winnie. 'I can't do magic to find the wand without having the wand to do the magic to find that wand that I can't do magic without. Oo, my head hurts!'

'Meow?' suggested Wilbur, pointing a paw above his head.

'Of course!' said Winnie. 'Great Aunt Winifred's wand will be in her trunk in the attic. I'll use that one.'

Winnie and Wilbur went up the grand staircase —**clomp! clomp!**— up the spindly spiral stairs—**clankety clang!** —then up the wobbly rope ladder— **whoops!**—to push open the trap door— **creak!**—and climb up into the dark attic where things squeaked and scuttled.

There was a big musty fusty old trunk
in a corner.

'Great Auntie's trunk!' said Winnie.
She lifted up the lid—**creak!** Then
she plunged a hand into the trunk, and
brought out Great Aunt Winifred's . . .
best bloomers. **'Euch!'**

Winnie's fingers felt around in the trunk some more and brought out ...

'Great Auntie's wand!' said Winnie. 'Ooer, it does look a bit old-fashioned, doesn't it. Do you think it still works?'

The wand *did* work, but in an old-fashioned way. When Winnie wanted better light to help her to climb down the wobbly ladder she waved the old wand, *'Abracadabra!'*

60

And instantly there were flickering
candle flames all over the attic.

'They'll set the house on fire!' said
Winnie. **Puff! Puff!** 'This whacky old
wand is just too old-fashioned, Wilbur.
I need a modern one.'

So Winnie went to her computer, and—**click! click!**—found Wendel's Wonderful World of Wands where she ordered the Silver Streak 13MXIII wand that had all the very latest features.

Ding dong! Ping pong! Sing a song!

'That's the doorbell,' said Winnie, hurrying downstairs. 'Witchmail is super fast!' She opened the door.

'Miss W. Watch?' asked the postman.

'It's *Witch*, not Watch!' said Winnie. 'Festering figs, do I look like a watch?'

'Well,' said the postman. 'You do have a face and two hands. Ha! Ha!'

'Do you want to be turned into a frog postman?' said Winnie.

63

'Er,' said the postman. 'No, Miss. Silly of me to say that. Could you please sign here, Miss Whatever-your-name-is?'

'Wow!' said Winnie as she drew the slender silver sparkling wand from the package. 'Look at all those buttons flashing, Wilbur!'

The first button Winnie tried made the wand invisible.

'Where's it gone?' said Winnie.

But then the wand let her know exactly where it was by poking her bottom. It reappeared, and made Winnie jump because it spoke.

'Oo,' said Winnie, licking her lips. 'I would like a big squidgy chocolate puffball filled with onion cream and sprinkled with sugared ants.' She waved the wand. *'Abracadabra!'*

But—**plonk!**—it wasn't a chocolate puffball that instantly arrived.

66

'That would not have been wise,'
explained the silver wand. 'I have replaced
your order with a healthier option. I hope
that you find it acceptable.'

'A carrot! I'm not a rotten rabbit,
you know!' said Winnie. 'Humph! I'm
going to magic my lovely old scruffy
wand back!' She waved the silver wand.
'Abracadabra!'

But the new wand knew better about that wish too.

'Oh no, Mistress,' it hissed. 'No, no, no. You mustn't replace me. Emphatically *no*.'

'But I don't want you!' Winnie threw the wand as far as she could but it just swerved around and came back to her.

68

She shoved the wand into a drawer and slammed it shut but the drawer slid back open, and the silver wand flew to Winnie again.

'Oh, you can't lose me, Mistress!' said the silvery wand. 'Oh, no, no!'

'Go away!' said Winnie.

'Hiss!' said Wilbur.

'Run for it!' said Winnie.

Winnie and Wilbur fled from the
house, slamming the door behind them.
Winnie stopped in the garden. 'What are
we going to do now?' wailed Winnie, and
she clutched at her head in despair. 'Oh, if
only I had my . . .' and suddenly Winnie
felt something thin and hard and long in
her hair, holding it all up. 'My old wand!'
Winnie pulled, and her hair tumbled.
'I didn't lose it after all!'

70

Just then—**crash!**—Winnie's door
flung itself open and the silver wand came
streaking towards them.

'Help!' said Winnie, holding her dear
old wand out as if it was a sword.

71

Soon she was—**crick! crack!**—
crossing wands with the silver wand.
Sparks flew, and splinters came off the dear
old wand. Then there was a deafening cry.

'Mrroww!' Wilbur ran from the house
with Great Aunt Winifred's wand. All
three wands battled together until—
crack!—one of them fell to the ground.
Winnie peeped between her fingers. The
silver wand had cracked in two. It wasn't
fizzing. It wasn't talking.

'Phewy!' said Winnie. 'I'm going to give that silver wand a new job to do. I do hope that it finds it acceptable!'

'Me-he-he!' laughed Wilbur as Winnie pinned her hair back up with a criss-cross of silver sticks.

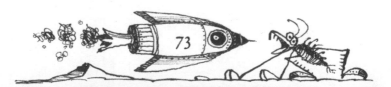

Spooky
WINNIE

One morning, at the end of October, Mrs
Parmar came calling at Winnie's house.

'**Winniiee!**' yelled the dooryell.

'I have something for you,' said Mrs
Parmar, putting an envelope into Winnie's
hand. 'The children and I thought it might
suit you.'

'What might suit me?' asked Winnie.
But Mrs Parmar was already hurrying
away.

'Meeow?' asked Wilbur.

'I've no idea at all,' said Winnie. 'Let's open it, and see.'

Winnie pulled out a card that read:

A Spiders, Spells and Spectres
SPECTACULAR

A HALLOWEEN PARTY
At the school tonight
Come in Spooky Fancy Dress
PLEASE
Bring decorations and food.

Winnie couldn't read all the words, but the children's pictures on the card helped her to understand.

'Whoopy doop, Wilbur! A Halloween party! We must get ready to go as soon as it gets dark tonight.'

'Let's make some decorations,' said Winnie. She whipped out her wand and waved it. '*Abracadabra!*'

Instantly there appeared a flock
of flapping black bats. They sorted
themselves into a line, held tiny bat
hands, and kicked their legs into a jig.
Bat bunting!

'Oh, they'll look lovely draped around
the school hall,' said Winnie. 'Especially
if they give a flutter and squeak every
now and again. I must bring some spiders

to make some spooky webs. We can
sprinkle the webs with glitter to look
pretty.' Winnie reached up to the top of
cupboards, and crouched down to look
under chairs, and ran her fingers along
floorboard cracks, picking up spiders.

'He he! They tickle!' she said. 'Now,
let's get Halloween cooking!'

Winnie and Wilbur looked at recipes, then they looked in the larder, and in the garden, and in the bin, and they collected ingredients. They chopped and chiselled and popped and topped and raked and baked. They made devilled gherkin ghastlies drizzled with real drizzle and dusted with real dust.

Slurp! Wilbur licked his lips.

WINNIIEE!

'They do look scrummy, don't they!' said
Winnie.

Outside it was getting dark. The moon
was shining. So were the stars.

'A perfect Halloween!' said Winnie.

'**Winniiee!**' yelled her dooryell again.

'Who ever can that be?' wondered Winnie.

'Oh, I should have said "what" ever instead of "who" ever!' said Winnie, because, there, on her doorstep, stood a little-ordinary devil and a little-ordinary ghoul.

'Trick or treat?' shouted the devil and the ghoul together, and they held out a pumpkin bucket that was already half full of sweets.

'I can choose, can I? Oh, goody goose
pimples!' said Winnie. 'Hmm. Well, I
think I'll do a trick then, thank you.'
Winnie waved her wand then pointed
it at the little-ordinary devil and the
little-ordinary ghoul, and she shouted,
Abracadabra!'

And, instantly, there were two little toads, sitting on her doorstep. 'Will that do?' asked Winnie.

'Croak! Croak!' said the ex-devil and the ex-ghoul. Fat toady tears began to fall down their warty green cheeks.

'Oh, dear!' said Winnie. 'Was that the wrong sort of trick for you? Do you want me to try something else?'

'Meow.' Wilbur whisper-explained to Winnie.

'Really?' said Winnie. 'Are you sure? *They* wanted to do a trick on *me*, did they? But wouldn't they like to stay as toads for the party?'

'Meeow!' Wilbur shook his head.

'All right, keep your fur on! I'll do it!' Winnie waved her wand again. '*Abracadabra!*'

Instantly the devil and the ghoul reappeared, running away as fast as they could.

'See?' said Winnie. 'They didn't want to do anything to me after all. Now what about my Halloween costume? It needs to be spooky and it must go with having a black cat, because you're coming to the party too, Wilbur. Any ideas?'

Winnie got out her dressing-up box. 'I've been told that I'm batty,' she said, 'so how about a bat costume?'

The bat suit was far too small and far too tight. 'I'm squeezed as tight as toothpaste in a tube! This is no blooming good!'

So Winnie and Wilbur threw on a couple of sheets, and tried being ghosts.

Trip-bang! 'I can't see where I'm going,' said Winnie, 'and I can't see to take food from a plate. Being a ghost is no good at all!' They threw off their sheets.

'Oh, if only there was something spooky that really suited a lady and a black cat!'

'Meow?' suggested Wilbur, holding up a

loo roll.

'The Egyptian-mummy look.' said
Winnie. 'Great! Wrap me up, Wilbur!'

Wilbur wound loo roll round and round
Winnie.

'Ooo, Wilbur!' said Winnie, her voice
muffled by loo paper. 'I can't move!'

So Wilbur pulled off the loo roll,

making Winnie spin like a top. 'Oh dear, I don't know what else I can try!' said dizzy Winnie.

'**Winniiee!**' yelled her dooryell *again*.

This time a little-ordinary skeleton and a little-ordinary ghost stood on the doorstep.

'Boo!' said the little ghost.

'Boo who?' said Winnie.

'Don't cry!' said the little ghost.

'Oh, very funny!' said Winnie. 'Are you going to the party? Can we come with you?'

So Winnie and Wilbur went to the party dressed as plain old Winnie and plain old Wilbur, taking their food and decorations with them.

91

'Come in, come in!' said Mrs Pumpkin
Parmar when they got to the school.
'Come and join in the fun.'

There was apple bobbing.

And pin the cat on the broomstick.

'Mrrrow!' said Wilbur.

There was dancing to the Bony Band of
Skeletons.

'Don't stand still, Mrs Parmar!' said
Winnie. 'My spiders are making webs
on anything that stays still for a single
maggoty-moment! Dance to keep them off
you!'

So even Mrs Parmar joined in with the
dancing. Winnie and Wilbur went wild.

It was a hauntingly-horribly-happy Halloween party. And it ended with prizes for the best costumes, awarded by the headmaster. There were prizes for the best pumpkin, the best ghost, the best ghoul, the best skeleton, and the best witch.

'Your costume was quite a good effort,' the headmaster told Winnie. 'But not as good as this little witch, I'm afraid.' And he gave the prize to a little-ordinary witch.

'Humph!' said Winnie.

94

But then she found that her gherkin
ghastlies hadn't all been eaten at the party.
So she and Wilbur went home happily
chomping ghastlies and spotting spooks as
they walked home through the Halloween
night.

Enjoy more magic moments with
Winnie AND **Wilbur**

KORKY